Kingdom
of the
Last Dragons
The Farloft Chronicles Vol. 2

Theresa Snyder

DEDICATION

For my Sarah

CONTENTS

BOOKS BY THERESA SNYDER

The Farloft Chronicles
(Fantasy)

James & the Dragon - Vol. 1
Kingdom of the Last Dragons - Vol. 2
Dragon Deception - Vol. 3
Too Many Dragons - Vol. 4
Three & a Half Dragons - Vol. 5

The Star Traveler Series
(Science Fiction)

The Helavite War - Vol. 1
The Heirs of Henu - Vol. 2
Old Friends/New Enemies - Vol. 3
The Malefactors - Vol. 4
Cataclysm - Vol. 5
A Mear Sleight of Hand - Vol. 5

Twin Cities Series
(Paranormal)

Shifting in The Realms

Learn more at:
www.TheresaSnyderAuthor.com

1 THERESA – THE HEALER

I am the Healer in the Village of Brownbriar at the foot of Westridge in the shadow of King William's castle.

I wrote James & the Dragon after my friend, Farloft, told me the story upon my return to the kingdom.

I am home now to stay and this is the continuing saga of James, Farloft and their adventures in The Kingdom of the Last Dragons, as I remember them.

2 JAMES' FLYING LESSON

I heard James shriek as he fell over the edge of the cliff. The shriek turned into a whoop of joy and a babble of laughter when his wings popped open and he started to soar. There is no experience quite as exciting as watching a fledging dragon learning how to fly.

I turned to Farloft and smiled. "How is James coming along?"

Farloft drew his eyes back from James' silhouette in the sky high above. "He is doing very well considering his background. He had a late start," the dragon apologized for James.

Farloft and I were sitting on his favorite perch – a sunny spot on a slab of rock just above the mouth to his cave. I heard his nails bite into the stone below us and followed his gaze up to James as he tumbled willy-nilly out of the sky – half flying, half falling.

"Feel the air," Farloft said softy under his breath, as he stared up. "Catch the wind." James continued to first drift then fall like a giant fat leaf in a stiff breeze. "POP," Farloft shouted at James. "Here comes the ground," he warned.

James struggled to right himself, his wings wrapped around him in a tangled mess. I heard Farloft's nails again and his own wings started to lift. At that instance one of James' wings caught the wind. It flipped him right side up and the other wing came out. He missed a head on collision with the ground by no less than 25 feet. James gave a cry of glee as he skimmed across the valley floor brushing his iridescent green belly, with hints of red, on the tops of the tall grass.

Farloft released his tension on the rock ledge and settled back into a sitting position, his wings falling gently back into place at his sides.

James made a long gradual turn and headed back across the valley toward the cliff face gaining a bit of altitude as he approached us.

I certainly wasn't going to be the one to tell Farloft, a dragon of over 1,000 years old how to teach another to fly, but James' approach looked somewhat like a battering ram on its way to impact.

"Is he going to make it?" I asked.

"Nope," Farloft stated flatly. "He has totally forgotten the warning I gave him about down drafts."

I heard a growl from down below and leaned over the ledge just in time to see James hit the cliff wall head first and fall about 50 feet to the ground.

Farloft didn't even move this time. He just shook his head in disappointment. I guess he didn't think a fall from that height would do much damage to the young dragon.

"Farloft," James called from below. "I forgot the downdraft," he apologized.

Farloft didn't repeat the obvious. He just sat there.

"Farloft?" James called again. "I don't think I can…"

Farloft grinned and looked at me. "He's only done launches from the cliff. No ground recovery."

"Oh my," I said. This was going to be interesting. A young dragon weighs a lot. More than your farm wagon, fully loaded, and its team of oxen combined. It takes experience to get that kind of bulk up in the air from a flat surface.

Farloft walked to the edge and looked down at James. "Either you are going to have to walk up the mountain or you will have to get the wind under you enough to catch air," he shouted.

We spent the next hour watching James run across the ground flapping his wings feverishly trying to 'catch the air.' By the time the sun was setting and I was ready to head for home James had given up and was sitting despondently on a huge rock at the bottom of the cliff. He didn't want to give up and climb the trail up the mountain like we humans.

"Is there a trick to it?" I asked Farloft as I rose to my feet.

"Yep," Farloft said with another toothy grin. "You have to face into the wind."

I mounted my horse and waved goodbye. I thought if James hadn't made it up by the time I passed him in an hour or so, I might, just might remind him of the secret of flight – into the wind.

3 SARAH'S VISIT

My niece, Sarah, is coming to visit. I have not seen her since my return from the Far East. She was eight when I left. Now I believe she will be 19 soon, if my calculations are correct. We used to look forward to her visits Garth and I. We never had children of our own.

I hope she will not find this stay a disappointment. Garth's death while we were aboard left me with few options. I no longer have rooms in the castle – just the little cottage by the river. But, I am anxious to see her. Joseph, the handyman, has built her a new bed and I have put needle to thread to produce a fine new mattress with clean white ticking and fresh fragrant straw. I rearranged the main room to give her a corner by the hearth. I hung a lovely piece of fabric from my travels up to give her privacy at night. It is what the people in the far east call 'silk.' The color is very vibrant and sheer. It makes the cottage seem bright and airy.

Farloft and James came by yesterday. They don't usually venture this way from their home. It is too close to human habitants. Farloft is afraid for James' safety due to the ever present danger of marauding knights in arms. However, he made an exception because I told him of Sarah's impending visit. He brought me a fine stag. I paid Joseph for his handy work with a hindquarter and will still have plenty to cook and store for my company.

Oh, I do hope Sarah enjoys her stay.

4 SARAH'S ARRIVAL

"Sarah?" I said in surprise when I caught a glimpse of her standing under the tree in front of my cottage. "Sarah, is that you?" I'd just returned from a visit with Maderia of the Forest Folk.

"Aunt T," Sarah exclaimed and ran into my arms. "I am so happy you are home." Sarah turned to her companion. "This is Todd, my father's dear friend. He offered to accompany me here."

I nodded my head in greeting. "Please, come inside. Supper is almost ready. I left it simmering while I was out with a patient."

Todd stayed for the evening meal, but then excused himself. He needed to continue on his own business. I thanked him for his safe delivery of Sarah and gave him a bit of the stag for his travels.

"Do you like it? Will it do?" I asked hopefully, as I held back the fabric to show Sarah her little corner of the cottage I prepared.

"It's perfect, Aunt T." She fingered the material from her seat on the new bed. "This is lovely."

I saw wonder in her eyes at the smooth texture of the fabric. She is a lovely child. I suppose I should not refer to her as a child. After all, she is 19, but seeing her after all these years made me feel so old. If Garth and I had borne children they would have been Sarah's mother's age and I would have grandchildren Sarah's age. It makes my head spin.

"Tomorrow we will let you rest from your journey, but the next day we shall see what mischief we can get into in the village," I promised her. A visit to see Laval, the Master Wizard, would be enlightening. I haven't seen him since my return. I have been meaning to drop by. I need to borrow some supplies if he can spare them.

5 AN AUDIENCE WITH LAVAL

Laval took Sarah's extended hand and bowed graciously. "I am pleased to meet you, Maid Sarah."

A light blush colored Sarah's cheeks. "It is my honor, Master Wizard."

"Please," Laval said as he motioned to a group of chairs by the fire. It was still cold in the castle during the early spring. "Would you care for a glass of wine?"

"Thanks you, that would be nice," I responded.

Sarah shook her head. "No, thank you."

Laval poured us a glass and then settled into the chair across from ours. "It has been a long time, Theresa. I had heard you were back from the East, but it is hard for me to get away. The King has not been well this past winter." I frowned and was about to speak when he went on. "Not the plague. That seems to have subsided. It is just old age, I am afraid. Soon he will be passing the crown on, I fear."

I knew the king had a son and a daughter. The daughter was the eldest, but the tradition was to pass the crown on to the male heirs. "Will it be William then?" I asked.

"Yes. There is no question, but with that decision there will be protest. William is not liked in this kingdom. It is not that he is cruel or even badly schooled; it is that he is indifferent to the people of his kingdom. He thinks only of himself and his own comforts. He is not a King to lead his people. He is a boy and will always be a boy even though he has passed his 20th year." Laval shook his head "I have tried to be available to him when he needs advice, but he never seeks it. He is so sure he is right in everything." Laval sipped at his wine. "But, let us not speak of politics. Tell me Theresa, what wonders have you seen in the East."

"It is a truly mystical place, Laval. I have returned with much more knowledge than I left behind. They are far advanced in the medicines. At first I was shocked and unbelieving of their methods, but I soon learned most of what I knew needed to be discarded. Their teachings proved themselves over and over again as I watched patients that would have floundered or died here, heal and flourish there."

"And do you intend to treat again in the village?" Laval asked.

In the past when I lived here I treated the villagers while he took care of the castle folks. "I do." I took a sip of my drink. "I do not know how well I will be received, but I used to have many who came to me for help prior to my leaving."

"And, do you intend to study with your aunt?" Laval asked Sarah.

"I am not sure I have the talent for a healer," she answered.

"Sarah is an artist." I smiled at her and she dropped her eyes to her lap – so shy. "I thought you might be able to arrange for her an introduction to the King for a portrait sitting, but now perhaps it would be better if it was with William."

"I am sure William would be delighted to sit for a portrait. There is nothing he likes more than attention," Laval said. "I will see what I can arrange."

"If it is not too much to ask, I need a favor too," I said. "I am looking for some swamp weed. It is out of season and not having been here last year to collect it in season, I have none. I wondered if you might loan me some. I would gather extra when it blooms for you when I pick mine this year."

"Of course, you have someone with a sour stomach you are treating?" Laval asked.

"More like a permanently sour disposition," I smiled, "the blacksmith. His wife asked me to see what I could do. Short of getting him to stop drinking, I don't hold out too much hope. But, I told her I would try."

"Of course, I'll go fetch it right now so we don't forget it. I must admit I have been distracted lately." Laval changed his tone. "You knew I lost my daughter, Megan, this past winter?"

"Oh, no – Laval. I had not heard." Laval and his daughter were very close. At a very young age, before my travels, she had shown an interest and a talent for wizardry. "Was it the plague?"

"Yes, and that damn stubborn dragon, Farloft. If it had not been for his procrastination I am sure I could have saved her." Laval set down his glass and walked to the fire. He turned his back to us and acted as though he were warming his hands before the fire. I knew him well enough to know he was trying to gather his control back. He was very upset with Farloft.

Funny Farloft had not said a word about Megan during our recent visit. I will have to ask him about what transpired.

6 FARLOFT'S MISTRUST

"You didn't mention Megan's passing last time we were together," I said. Farloft looked down at me. I stopped by after dropping off a potion to Maderia. "I saw Laval a few days ago. He is very upset with you. I know you haven't been friends for a long time, but he blames you for Megan's death. What actually happened while I was away?"

Farloft unfurled his wings, stretching them up to their full length. He was thinking. I have set many times in the past and waited for his thoughts to congeal. He looked up at James making lazy circles in the sky. The young dragon was flying with a lot more confidence. He would be old enough for fireworks soon. As it was, he left a faint trail of smoke in the air – being unable to control his smoldering inner fire at this point.

I put my hand on Farloft's leg and stroked. It was not a necessarily pleasing sensation for me – he was scaly, but I knew the dragon liked to be touched. He had been alone for many years prior to James' arrival. He was the only one I was reluctant to leave when Garth asked if we should go east to study. I knew if I left, Farloft would be alone.

"I have not been able to trust Laval since his treachery many years ago. I let that mistrust cloud my judgment. When the plague took our kingdom hostage, he came to me for help and I refused. I should have seen he was honestly seeking my assistance at that time. Later when he returned to ask again and told me Megan was ill, I gave him what he wanted. By then it was too late - too late for Megan - too late for our past friendship to rekindle. As always he turned sour and plotted against me. It is only through James' swift action I was spared. My opinion of the wizard has not changed. He cannot be trusted."

For Farloft, the greatest teller of tales I have ever heard, this was not a clear explanation. It was filled with big gaps of information I longed to know. What sort of plot misfired on the wizard? I knew James was once a boy from the village and Laval somehow changed him into the young dragon he now was. How did James *save* Farloft and from what? You can never rush Farloft. He gives his information, or tells his stories, at his own speed. I would have to wait until he was ready to divulge the full story.

"Did you see me?" James asked with a huge toothy grin as he landed on the ledge beside Farloft. He had a bit too much momentum and slid into the adult dragon. Farloft was so much larger than James he didn't even move.

"Your flying is progressing, but you still need work on your landings," Farloft said, as he nudged James playfully with his nose. "And, by the looks of that smoke trail you were leaving, you are not breathing correctly yet."

"Breathe in, bank left, down drafts...There is a lot to learn, Farloft," James complained. "I thought I was doing pretty good...Did you see that spiral I did?" Even in the short time I had known James I realized he lived for the older dragon's compliments.

"Yes, indeed I did and it was very nicely done...Couldn't have done better myself," Farloft said. At this point James' stomach growled. It sounded like a cross between a huge dog and a bass drum. "I hope you will excuse us, Theresa. It seems my young protégé is in need of a meal." James took this as a signal to take flight again. He dropped over the edge of the cliff and spiraled out into the void.

"Don't let me keep you," I said as I got to my feet. "We will have plenty of time to talk now that I am home. No need to keep a young dragon waiting for his supper."

Farloft lowered his head. He huffed gently into my hair causing a warm sensation down the whole length of my body. "It is good to have you back, Healer. Come again soon."

7 ASSAULT ON SARAH

I turned when Sarah crashed through the door of the cottage. Her hair was loose and in her eyes. Her face was red as though she had been running – hard.

"Sweetheart, what has happened?"

She stood in the doorway. "It fell. It crashed right beside me." She gestured back out the door behind her. "That whole end of the field has a huge furrow plowed down it." She buried her face in her hands and shook her head. "I think it's hurt."

I took her by the hand and lead her to the hearth. "Sit down and tell me what happened. What fell? Who is hurt?"

She plopped down, exhausted. I poured her a glass of water as she tried to gather her thoughts.

"I was sitting on a rock drawing that lovely tree at the edge of Mr. McGonagall's field. You know the one I spotted on the way to the castle the other day?" I nodded. "I was just sitting there, drawing and I heard this very loud sound right behind and above me." She concentrated. "It was like a sheet caught in a stiff wind. Then there was this whoosh of air and the dragon fell right in front of me. It slid for several yards." She took the glass I offered and gulped down some water. "I ran up to it. It opened its eyes. They were huge. The most beautiful green..." Her voice slowed and she looked lost. "They had little copper flecks in them. They..." I touched her arm and she seemed to come back from far away. "It's hurt, Aunt T. It sprang up, but it limped and when it flew away it looked unbalanced. Like its wing was hurt."

It had to be James. "Did you see any blood?" I asked. "Any arrows or spears?"

"No." Sarah shook her head. "I don't think it was attacked. I think it was hurt in the fall."

"You didn't see anyone else around?"

"No." she said thoughtfully. "You don't think it was going to attack me, do you?"

"Of course not, sweetheart. I am relatively sure it was James. He is young and just learning to fly. I think he probably over shot his mark." I brushed her hair out of her eyes. "Are you all right? You weren't hurt?"

"I'm fine," she said as she brushed my hand aside. "You didn't tell me there was a dragon here."

"I'm sorry, I didn't think to tell you. The villagers don't see much of them. They usually keep to themselves."

"There is more then one?" Sarah asked in disbelief. I am so used to Farloft and James, I forgot there were no dragons in the kingdom where she was raised.

"Yes, there are two. Farloft a dragon that has lived here for over a thousand years and James, a boy with a spell case upon him that changed him into a dragon just last year." I smoothed back Sarah's hair again and tucked it gently behind her ear. "Are you sure you are alright?"

"It just scared me. I've never seen a dragon before. I was going to see if it was all right when it just sprang up and took off." Her face took on that far away look again. "You think it was James?...His eyes were so beautiful - such an incredible shade of green with copper flecks. They were so deep." She looked up from her glass. "We should go check on him. I know he was hurt."

I rose and pulled my healer's bag from off the shelf. It was time she met Farloft and James. "Gather your cloak. It will be cold by the time we get there. We'll go up and see if my talents are needed."

Sarah grabbed her cape and was out the door before

I settled my cloak over my shoulders.

8 DAZZLERS AND DRAGONS

Farloft greeted me in front of his cave. "He's embarrassed. He doesn't want to see you. I already offered to fetch you."

"How bad are his injuries?" I asked.

"Both his paws are scraped and he hit his chin, but it is the tear in his wing I am concerned about. If it gets much worse, he won't be able to fly."

Sarah cleared her throat behind me.

"Oh, pardon me. Farloft, this is my niece, Sarah."

Sarah stepped out from the shadow of the rock face behind me and into the light of the setting sun.

"It's pretty," Farloft said in a soft voice.

"IT is a girl, Farloft. Sarah, my niece," I repeated.

Farloft raised his paw very slowly and placed the tip of his pointing claw on the barrette in Sarah's hair. The light of the setting sun was reflected off the silver and bits of shiny glass it was made from. "It's a pretty Dazzler. I can see why it caught his eye. He said he didn't realize it was attached to a girl until it was almost too late."

"You haven't told James about a dragon's attachment to sparkling things?" I asked in surprise. Dragon's were absolutely mesmerized by shiny things if Farloft was any example. "Farloft?" The big dope just stood there staring at Sarah's barrette.

She reached up, took the barrette out of her hair and slid it into her pocket.

Farloft seemed to come to his senses again. "Well, not in so many words. I have kept him out of my hoard chamber since his transformation, but there didn't seem to be any need to go into Dazzlers in detail since I was keeping him away from the castle and the villagers don't have anything so fine."

"Well, you certainly should have," I reprimanded. "He could have taken her head off."

"Well, I had no idea she would be foolish enough to wear a Dazzler in the middle of a field, during the day," Farloft argued back.

"It's only made of pot metal and glass, Farloft. The only ones attracted to it would be a dragon," I retorted.

Sarah shook her head and pushed her way through

the two of us to enter the cave. Farloft and I fell silent. We poked our heads around the corner of the cave to watch as Sarah approached James. James was lying curled up on the floor. His tail wrapped around him and his wings stretched out over him like a huge protective tent. Sarah stopped right in front of him. He opened his eyes and saw her. He got up and shifted his position so he had his back to her. She circled around in front of him again. He rose once more and turned his back on her again. He curled himself in the tightest ball he could manage. She came around again and this time before he could move, she grabbed his muzzle between her hands and held him still.

"I understand you saved my life," She said. "I wanted to thank you."

"I almost killed you," James mumbled between her hands.

"But, as you can see, you didn't." Sarah released her hands. "My name is Sarah. Theresa, the Healer, is my aunt." James didn't say a word. "I am visiting for a while. I have never been in a dragon country. I didn't know about your attraction to shiny things. Do you have a hoard?"

"Not yet, but Farloft has a huge collection. It was all

given to him. We don't steal things like human's think." James explained. "I thought your barrette was lying in the grass. I didn't see you were attached to it until I got up close," he apologized.

"I always heard dragons had exceptional eyesight."

"Oh, we do," James seemed to be warming to his subject. "I was just Dazzled, Farloft said - just really focused on your shiny barrette."

"Have you thought about starting a hoard of your own?" Sarah asked.

"I have today," James confessed.

"Where would you put it?" Sarah asked.

"Let me show you," James said, rising to his feet.

"Lead on, Sir James," Sarah said, with a curtsy in his direction.

James stopped in his tracks. "Why did you call me that?"

"I don't know. Maybe because you saved my life," Sarah said. "If I were a princess, I would knight you."

James smiled. "Well then, this way my lady."

Sarah followed him deeper into the cave. Farloft and I followed behind. It is difficult to be sneaky with a dragon the size of a small castle at your side, but I don't think James and Sarah minded the company. James led us to a small chamber down the main tunnel. It was just big enough for him and Sarah. Not large enough for the four of us to squeeze inside. It was a rock formation reminiscent of a geode with one side missing. The crystals on the floor of the chamber had been worn down to dust over the centuries, but the sides and ceiling were covered with crystals that ranged in color from clear in the center of the ceiling to a deep purple at the base of the walls. One of the many volcanic tubes in the mountain came to the surface on one side of the chamber and the glow from the molten lava down in its depths lit the chamber and made it sparkle like a room of jewels.

"This is a Dazzler in itself," Sarah said, using the dragon's term. "It is lovely." Sarah turned slowly in a complete circle and took it all in. When she stopped, she was facing James. "I would like us to be friends, James." Sarah took her barrette out of her pocket and laid it on the floor. "I will make you a gift of this Dazzler and it will be the first of your own hoard."

James' eyes turned from a soft mint green to a deep

emerald shade. The flecks of copper in them seemed to float. He managed to tear his eyes off the barrette long enough to say thank you. I believe this will be a long friendship. Perhaps as long as Farloft's and mine.

9 JAMES' INJURED PRIDE

I spread the glutinous mixture on James' wing. "No flying for two days and then just sailing for another two days," I instructed. In my experience I have found dragons heal quickly. The tear was not bad.

I moved around to his paws and spread more of the salve I brought with me on the scrapes. I lifted his chin to spread some on a raw spot. When I let go, he lowered his head and a huge tear ran down his cheek.

"I'm sorry. Did I hurt you?" I asked.

"No, I…" His explanation fell silent.

"What is it, James? Are you hurt somewhere else?"

He nodded his head.

"Where?" I started to circle him looking for another injury.

"I…I broke a tooth," He said. I came around him and he opened his massive jaws to reveal a broken canine. "I haven't told Farloft."

"Oh, you silly." I took his muzzle in my hands. The muzzle of a dragon is the only think that is soft on them. There are small fibers on each scale – perhaps they have something to do with the fire process, but they are soft like the nose of a horse. "Dragon's live a very long time, James. You will go through many sets of teeth. When your body realizes this one is not doing you any good, it will reject it and you will grow another," I explained.

James smiled a toothy, lopsided grin. "There is so much I don't know about being a dragon. Do you think I will ever learn?"

"Farloft is the best teacher you could have, James, and you have a long time to learn." I patted him on the nose. "Let's go see what the big guy has caught for dinner – shall we?"

James' stomach rumbled deeply in answer to my question.

10 FARLOFT'S FAVORITE TREASURE

Sarah and I spent the night in Farloft and James' cave. It was too late to make our way down the mountain in the dark. Farloft took us to the inner cave. It is a larger version of James' hoard chamber. However, it has a pool in the middle heated by the same volcanic vents that light all the chambers. Sarah and James waded in the shallows as Farloft and I visited.

"She is a charming young lady," Farloft said, as he studied Sarah.

Sarah splashed James and came running over to join us.

"Farloft? What was the first piece of your hoard?" Sarah asked, as she plopped down beside me. She dried her legs with the hem of her skirt.

"Yes, Farloft, what was it?" James asked. He laid down across from us, his head propped on his paws.

Farloft thought for a moment. "That has been so long ago, I am not sure I remember."

"You always remember everything, Farloft," James

said. "Come on."

Farloft frowned. "It was a small shiny piece of metal from a suit of armor - not nearly as fine an object as yours, James." The older dragon smiled at Sarah.

"What's your favorite piece in your treasure, Farloft?" Sarah asked.

"Ah, now that's another story." Farloft stretched out on the sand. He was getting comfortable, and knowing him, James and I settled down for a tale. The older dragon carefully reached up and lifted a large scale on his chest. With two of his claws on his other paw he reached under the scale and removed a large emerald. He started to hand it to James.

"No, I'll drop it and it will get lost in the sand," James said.

I held out my hand. It had to be extremely valuable to Farloft if he carried it on him all the time. I held it in my open palm as Sarah and I admired it. James turned a bit glassy eyed, but managed to keep focused enough to listen to the older dragon's story.

"I was a youngish dragon a few centuries ago when dragons and humans were partners and sometimes good friends." Sarah moved over by James and leaned up against the young dragon's side. "I was assisting the King in his battle against the Hillerst. The enemy had made it to the very walls of the castle. The King's men were greatly outnumbered. There was an imminent chance the palace would be overrun. I was on the tower when the queen came to me." Farloft went on. "She had her child with her – the future king. At that time he was only a toddler - maybe one or two year's olds. He would have been the great, great grandfather of our current King. The queen asked me to take her child to safety and care for him. I begged her to come with us, but she would not leave the King's side."

Farloft shifted a bit and looked over at Sarah. "I understand you may do Prince William's portrait. He is named after the child that was given to me to protect, Prince William I. His mother wrapped him in her fur and handed him up to me. The King urged me to go quickly – the enemy was advancing. I cradled him in my paw. He was so tiny, but I was soon to find that taking care of him was much more stressful than any battle I ever fought."

"I brought him here," Farloft said, as he indicated the chamber we were in with a flip of his tail. "I no sooner got him here than he soiled himself. It smelled worse than a week old carcass. You can imagine my difficulty in removing his nappy. These were not made for detailed work," Farloft said, as he held up his huge paw. "I washed him in the edge of the pool and held him over one of the heat vents to dry. He thanked me by 'doing it' again in the vent. However, that gave me an idea. I found out from that incident he 'did it' when he was warm and comfortable. Did you know babies make faces before they 'do it'?" Farloft asked.

Sarah and I both giggled.

"No, they do," the dragon assured us. "I would watch for that look and the grunting – when it came, I just held him over the vent and then rewrapped him in the fur after."

"Quite, clever," I complimented Farloft.

"Well, that was only one thing I had to overcome. Shortly after he 'did it' he started to cry. It took me some time to figure out he was hungry. I began to wonder what Queen Aktra had thought giving me the responsibility of her child. He was unrelenting. His squall was ear splitting. I realized I had no idea what a child his age ate. I knew milk was a staple for younglings of all kinds, so I placed Prince William in a former vent chamber that had long since gone dormant and went to find a nanny goat for the child." Farloft looked at James. "Can you imagine how difficult it was to catch a live goat?"

James laughed – a deep bass sound like rolling thunder in his throat. He had told us earlier what a time he had when Farloft took him to hunt.

"Here I was flying around swooping and turning, trying to corner a goat while I could hear and see the battle raging at the base of the castle. I would so much rather be among the troops. I finally caught it, but not without skinning my toes and knocking down a perfectly good barn by mistake."

We all giggled at the visual of the mighty dragon in his younger years and not near so talented.

"But how does all this lead to the favorite piece of your hoard?" Sarah asked.

"Wait for it," James cautioned. "Farloft eventually gets there."

"Quite right," Farloft said. "So, as I was saying, through great difficulty I brought the bleating goat back here. Of course, it was frightened and I had to stare it down. Dragons can stare other lesser animals into submission – though I wasn't very good at it in my earlier years. It takes practice. However, I did eventually get the darn goat to stand still.

"It was at this point that I realized William was not

where I left him. I searched frantically for the child. At first I feared he had drowned. I waded the pool from shore to shore and back again. Then I envisioned him climbing into one of the vents and falling to his death in the lava far below. I was frantic until I heard a giggle and the clink of silver."

"He made it all the way back to your hoard?" James asked in surprise. It was a long way down the tunnel to the chamber. James knew from experience. He lugged many a treasure out to the pool to shine for Farloft last winter during the snow that kept him stranded here. He was a boy then and it had been hard work.

"Indeed he did," Farloft said with a grin. "He was quite the adventurer. The minute he saw me his giggles turned to tears again. He knew I was the source of food if there was any. There was a further trial of getting William to figure out what the goat was for. I felt a bit sorry for the goat. The child was not very gentle with her and it was only after mauling her in frustration that he finally figured out he could get milk from her."

"I just got the situation under control and the child to sleep, when I heard horses outside. I was ready to defend the boy with everything I had, but there was no need. It was the King and his Queen. The battle swayed in his favor and the enemy was on the run. He left his second in command and came to fetch his son. I was able to hand over the child as good as he had been presented to me – short one nappy." Farloft took the stone from me and held it up to the light. "The King was still in full armor, having come straight from battle. He had nothing to give me for my services, so he took his dagger and pried a stone from his crown. This very stone."

Sarah admired the sparkle of the emerald. "Seems like your efforts were worth it."

"Yes, well worth it. It was wonderful when we all lived peacefully together."

"Maybe we can repair the breach that has grown between dragons and men," she said.

"It would be more than I have been able to do these past centuries, but we can always hope," Farloft said. He tucked the emerald back under the scale of his breast plate and settled down using his paws for a pillow. He shot a burst of dragon fire at the two nearby rock outcrops he was keeping heated for Sarah and my benefit as his eyes drifted closed he said in a soft voice, "we can only hope. Goodnight, ladies."

11 SARAH'S ART SUPPLIES

The next day Sarah met me as I dismounted from Knicker. "How are Maderia and her brood?" she asked.

I'd been to see Maderia of the Forest Folk again. I unhitched and pulled Knicker's saddle off. He helped by pulling off his blanket and tossing it over the stall railing. He nickered his satisfaction at being so clever. I patted him a thank you for his efforts.

"Several of them have ingested a toxic grass. I pointed it out to Maderia and she is going to have her people work to get it all pulled." I scooped up some grain in Knicker's bucket and put it on the hook in his stall. He thanked me with a light whinny. He is a very verbal horse, hence his name. I turned from putting him in his stall, "Come inside, I want to hear all about your visit with Prince William." I took Sarah's arm as we headed toward the cottage. I hung my cloak at the door as Sarah swung the kettle over the fire to start it boiling for tea.

"Was he nice? Did you like him? Is he going to have you do his portrait?" I asked with enthusiasm.

"Yes, Yes and Yes," Sarah said with a smile.

"Well, tell me all about it," I prompted. I pulled off my gloves and boots, and shoved my feet into my more comfortable slippers.

"I was escorted to his personal part of the castle. It is the East wing and has wonderful light. His parlor is a perfect place to set up and do the portrait." She stoked the fire up a bit. Dusk was falling and the cottage had a light chill in the air. I plumped the pillow in my chair and sat down by the fire to warm my hands. "He is incredibly handsome, Aunt T. It will be a pleasure to draw him. His features are chiseled and his hair has this unusual streak of silver in it from his forehead to just behind his right ear. It is very striking." Sarah had a far off look in her eye. It reminded me of James with his dazzler. "He seems a bit lost at the thought of becoming King. He loves his father very much." Her attention turned to me as I opened the tin and added the tea to the hot water in the kettle. "He talked about his father in detail. I think William is actually lonely."

"William?" I asked.

"He gave me permission to address him by his given name," Sarah said with a shy smile. "I am going to start his portrait as soon as I can gather the materials

I need."

I poured Sarah and myself a cup of tea. "What will you need, exactly?"

"William said I could speak to the monks about paper. I have some of my drawing implements with me. I may need more. Could we go to the market in Tellishire next gathering?"

"That is a wonderful idea. I need some things too. We can stop and visit with your Uncle Jeffory. He hasn't seen you since you were a toddler." I sipped my tea and envisioned my younger brother meeting his niece after so many years. He is an old curmudgeon, but nothing gets him out of that mood faster than a pretty young girl. "We should make plans and send a message to Jeffory that we are coming."

"I can make some trial sketches in the meantime of William. He is anxious to get the portrait finished before something happens to his father. He wants him to see it."

"Then it's settled. We make for Tellishire in less than a full moon's span." It is going to be so good to see my little brother, Jeffory.

12 CONCERNS FOR LAVAL

"I saw the crown today, Aunt T," Sarah said off handedly. We were sitting outside in front of the cottage in the afternoon sun. It had been almost a month since she started sketching Prince William. "It really is missing the stone Farloft carries. They have never replaced it." I was popping peas for dinner while Sarah worked over a trial sketch of Prince William. "I asked William what happened to the stone. Do you know he had no idea? I didn't tell him the story Farloft told us. Not that I don't believe Farloft, just that I didn't think it was my place." She erased the same part of her sketch again. "I can't get the mouth quite right."

"Keep at it," I said. "I have confidence in you or I wouldn't have introduced you to Laval."

"Speaking of Laval," she said. "He seems very preoccupied every time I see him. Prince William says he hasn't been the same since shortly after his daughter's death. The people at the castle say he is distant due to her passing, but somehow I think it is something else. He mumbles under his breath. I wonder if he is sane. Do you think the loss of Megan has driven him crazy?"

"Not Laval. He is too old and experienced a wizard. He has one of the strongest minds I know. I could look in on him prior to our departure next week. Do you think I should?"

"I would feel better if you did," Sarah said. "You are the only Healer other than Laval in the area. If he can't reach out to you, you need to go to him."

13 A SURPRISE ENCOUNTER WITH DRAGONS AND KNIGHTS

Sarah and I were on our way. In retrospect, I should have seen Laval before we left, but time got away from me. We rose before dawn and were off just as the sun peeked over the horizon. I wanted to make it to Jeffory's in one day - one very long day. We would most likely make it in time to have the cook warm us up some left over supper.

Knicker and Tolly, Sarah's piebald mare, were busy vying for first place on the road, both sending puffs of warm breath into the cool morning air when Farloft and James arrived unexpectedly. Farloft landed gently at Knicker's side with hardly a disturbance of the air. Knicker whinnied and tossed his head in irritation. Farloft blew a puff of smoke in his face and the horse shied away, thoroughly rebuffed. James' landing was noisier and involved a lot more dust. The two dragons hemmed Sarah and me in between them as we proceeded down the road.

"Lovely weather we are going to have today," Farloft said. He puffed at Knicker again.

"Stop that," I chastised him. "I'll never get him to like you if you blow smoke in his face each time you meet. Besides, I get the over spray and I don't want to smell like dragon breath when I get to Brother Jeffory's." Knicker snorted and blew in agreement with me. I swear if he had been a dragon, there would have been more than snorting going on between them.

Tolly was behaving herself nicely under Sarah. In fact, the young mare seemed as interested in James as her rider. "What brings you out so early," Sarah asked James.

"Just hunting and we saw you. Thought we would drop down and see where you were headed," James answered. His eyes were on Sarah when he stumbled over the bushes beside the road. His wings instinctively flew out to balance him. He would have knocked Sarah off her horse if she hadn't ducked just in time. She patted Tolly's neck to calm her as James got his feet firmly back under him and his wings folded by his sides. "Sorry," he apologized.

Sarah smiled at him. "It's all right. We're headed to my Uncle Jeffory's house in Tellishire, and we're going to the gathering while we are there," Sarah said with excitement.

"Sarah needs some supplies in order to complete Prince William's portrait," I explained.

James smiled his toothy grin. "So you did get the assignment?"

At that moment everything happened at once. I glimpsed Farloft cock his head to listen, then he threw himself across our path. I heard horse's hooves on the road coming fast. I heard, rather than saw, a burst of dragon fire just as Sarah shouted, "No, it's Prince William!" She was trying to urge Tolly between James and Farloft who had taken a stance directly in front of us. All I could see was Farloft's flank blocking my way. I kicked him in the side with my booted foot. It had about as much affect as attacking a grizzly bear with a toothpick, but it did get his attention.

"What is going on?" I demanded.

Sarah shouted, "It's Prince William and his men."

Over her Farloft snorted, "They are knights with drawn swords and crossbows."

I slipped off Knicker and dropped his reins to the ground so he would stay in one place during the bedlam. I slapped Tolly on the butt to get her out of the way and weeded my way through to the front.

Sure enough there sat Prince William on his horse, sword in one hand, shield in the other. His hair was a bit singed, other than that he seemed uninjured, just very angry. His men huddled protectively about him.

In a level tone I said, "Now let's all calm down."

"Sarah? Are you all right?" Prince William shouted.

"She was doing fine 'til you almost scared her to death charging us," James growled.

"Scared her?" Prince William retorted. "You were the ones attacking her."

"We…"

I broke into Farloft's denial. "No one was attacking," I said. "It is all a huge mistake. Please, sheath your sword young prince and have your men do the same," I requested. "Farloft, stand down please," I asked as I patted his front leg to further illustrate to the prince that we were all friends. Farloft didn't move, but did relax a bit.

Sarah slipped off her horse and came to William's side. "Please, we are all friends here," she told him.

William sat unmoving on his horse. "I am not friends with any dragons."

"Then perhaps you had best go back to whatever you were doing and leave us to proceed on our way. We were having a nice morning constitutional before you so rudely interrupted," Farloft stated aggressively in his deep baritone.

"Farloft," I reprimanded. "The Prince and his men only thought they were defending us."

"Because they only saw Monstrous Dragons," Farloft snorted a smoke puff in William's face.

William did his best not to cough, "I saw two ladies hemmed in by two dragons. It is not a normal sight," William defended his actions.

"Let me introduce you all properly," I suggested.

"I am not interested in making the acquaintance of any dragon," William rebuffed.

"Nor are we interested in meeting a spoiled brat of a Prince," Farloft snorted. "Come James, the air is a bit stale for my taste here." Farloft turned to Sarah and me and inclined his head, "Healer, Sarah." A swoosh of air and he was up.

James side stepped Sarah and the Prince. "See you," he said to Sarah. He loped forward on all fours until he could catch enough air to join Farloft in the sky above. They both tilted their wings in a goodbye salute and were gone.

Prince William sheathed his sword. "May we escort you ladies?" the Prince offered.

I shook my head. "We will be fine, your Highness. I am sure you were occupying your time elsewhere before you came upon us."

"We were out hunting, but we would be please to accompany you," he offered again and smiled down at Sarah affectionately.

I had really had enough of men for the day, be they dragon or human. "Thank you, your Highness, but we wouldn't think of taking you away from the hunt. We will be fine."

Sarah looked a bit disappointed in my refusal of an escort, but she backed away from Prince Williams' horse.

"Every well," William said in a somewhat dismissive tone. "As you wish." He took his reins in hand, motioned to his men and they rode off at a gallop.

"Well, that went well," Sarah said sarcastically.

14 VISIT TO TELLISHIRE

The rest of the trip was uneventful compared to the beginning. Sarah and I spent an inordinate amount of time reflecting on the stubbornness of males, both human and dragon.

Tellishire lies in a valley between two mountain ridges. The city is walled with a gate at the north and south ends of the valley. My brother Jeffory is the gatekeeper at the south gate and part-time scribe for the surrounding community. His home is a small, but cozy room above the gate. He was given the job when he left the monastery. He still wears his monk's robes and tries to live a spiritual life, but his beliefs and the churches parted long ago. Over the years I got so used to referring to him as Brother Jeffory. I still slip and address him thus.

Jeffory was at his post when we arrived, the gates having long since been closed for the night. He poked his head out the window above and smiled down at us. "I'll be right down," he said.

Once the horses were settled in the stable and we were seated with a bowl of hot stew and a cup of tea from the cook's provisions allotted to the gatekeeper, Sarah launched into her retelling of the auspicious start to our journey.

"Nothing more stubborn then a dragon to my way of thinking," Jeffory commented between mouthfuls. "From what Theresa tells me, Farloft has had more than a few years to learn disappointment from the hands of humans."

"He certainly has," I interjected. "People lump dragons all together, like they were all alike and inseparable. They are not anymore alike in character than I am to the King."

"Do we even know what started the distrust between them?" Sarah asked.

"In this kingdom it has always been a matter of disagreement between Farloft and Laval," I answered. "However, whatever that disagreement was has never been revealed to anyone that I know of. Neither Farloft nor Laval have ever spoken to me about it in the fifty odd years I have known them."

"I wonder if they even remember," Sarah asked.

"Dragons never forget," Jeffory said. He put his empty bowl to one side and picked up his flute. "How about a tune? I got this one off a visitor here for the gathering."

I settled back in my chair – tomorrow the gathering.

15 THE MARKET OF TELLISHIRE

Jeffory led Sarah to the illuminator's stalls where she purchased iron gall, walnuts and aged hawthorn for ink making. She assured the seller she knew the techniques of producing the finished product. She was just not sure which type of ink she wanted to use at this point. She spent ages picking out quills and reeds for the laying down of the ink. She would need to temper and sharpen the quills when we got home.

From the illuminator's stall Sarah migrated to the rug seller. She wanted to buy a rug for beside her bed. She had numerous selections laid out when Jeffory and I left her to go to the herbalist to purchase the items on my list. We picked up the dried herbs I needed to carry me over until I could gather my own this fall. When we returned to the rug seller's stall Sarah had narrowed her selection down to three of the original five she pulled out and added two new ones to her pile. She wanted to know which one I liked. I picked two and we left her to continue her struggle to make a decision.

Jeffory took my hand. His hands are always so

warm. His robes flapped in the breeze as we walked through the stalls of the gathering. I have always been amazed at how tall he is. He towers over me and unlike me is thin as a lodge post. If you dressed him in regular clothing, he would make a great scarecrow. We made our way to the local pub for some refreshments.

I sat down and put my feet up in the chair next to Jeffory's. "At this rate, we might get home before the winter snows set in," I said referring sarcastically to Sarah's split second decision on which rung to purchase.

"She's a thinker all right, watching her funds," Jeffory said, as he picked up his mug of mulled wine, "unlike her uncle who spends nothing or her aunt that spends like she is a wealthy land baroness."

"I spend what I can and will die happy doing it," I countered. "I thought you got over your disagreeable phase when you left the church."

"I did," he said. "However, I never get over my lecturing phase when I am around you."

"Oh, heaven help me."

The delivery of our meal put an end to any retort Jeffory may have had.

Sarah came in about a half hour later with her purchase under her arm. She rolled it out on the floor. "What do you think?" It was hand braided in shades of red, orange and yellow. "It reminded me of a sunrise."

"It will go nicely with the curtain dividing your area from the rest of the cottage," I agreed. "But, I thought you were leaning toward purchasing the blue one."

"Do you think I should have?" she asked. "I could take this one back."

"No, oh no," Jeffory and I answered almost in unison.

Sarah rolled the rug back up and took a seat. "I bought a little something for James. I have to put it together." She pulled some colorful glass beads, three shinny pieces of copper and some fine jute from her bag. "I found the beads at a small stall near the church. I'm going to hunt for a nice piece of wood on the way home and make him a wind chime. What do you think?"

"I think he will love it, though he may have to share it with Farloft," I said as I admired her choice of blue and amber beads.

"Bet the gent selling them never thought they would be given to a dragon," Jeffory said with a chuckle. "Beads for a dragon. Who would have thought?"

Sarah held up the beads strung on their string. "Dazzlers," she said with a satisfied smile.

16 ANOTHER CHANCE ENCOUNTER

Jeffory stood at Knicker's side with his hand on my boot. "I wish you would dress more like the lady you are."

"I wish you wouldn't lecture," I replied. I have dressed in trousers for years. Wearing pants lends well to my trade as a Healer. I do a lot of kneeling down to my patients, whether human or animal, in my business. "You know I am not going to change."

"And, funny as it may seem, that is exactly why I love you, sister," Jeffory said as he squeezed the toe of my boot. "Take care of yourself."

"I will," I promised.

"Come and see me again soon, young lady," Jeffory said to Sarah as she leaned over from Tolly's back to plant a kiss on his cheek.

"I will Uncle Jeffory. Thank you for letting us stay." Sarah turned Tolly's head toward the road home.

I had to lean down from Knicker's back to plant a kiss on the thinning hair of Jeffory's head. For a change, on Knicker's back I was taller than my little brother. "Take care, brother Jeffory."

We dallied on the way home. Talking about our visit and the interesting things we saw and did, we lost all track of time until the sun started to set and home was still several hours away. We were not prepared for a night on the road, but we had warm clothes and provisions Jeffory insisted we take. We picked the lea of a hill, under the shelter of a tall old oak to make camp for the night. We hobbled Knicker and Tolly nearby in a stand of sweet spring grass. Sarah and I found firewood easily, an old branch from the oak fallen during a storm long ago. Sarah spread her new rug as a bed for us. We pulled our cloaks about us and were quite content with our backs to the trunk of the huge ancient oak and the warmth of the fire in our faces.

It was a clear night so I saw Farloft and James coming and pointed them out to Sarah.

"Do you think they are out hunting this late?" Sarah asked.

"Yes, but not for what you think," I replied. Dragons can, and do, hunt at night sometimes. Their eyesight is incredible, something between a cat and an eagle combination, but I thought they were probably looking for us. My thoughts were proved correct when they landed.

"Thought we would join you for a spell," Farloft announced as he landed.

"Farloft saw your fire all the way from the cliff," James said in admiration.

"Just used to spotting things out of the ordinary," Farloft dismissed his extraordinary sight. He lowered his head to come under the tree partway and then laid down much like a huge green dog with his head on his paws. James followed suit from the other side. The two of them created a scaly green wall between the fire and the countryside. Sarah and I would be snug as bugs on her new rug.

"How was your visit?" Farloft asked.

"It was good to see brother Jeffory." I tossed another piece of wood on the fire. "He doesn't look like he has aged a year since I left."

"Was the gathering fun?" James asked. "I always wanted to go when I was…younger. I mean, it sounds like fun. I've heard there are jugglers and…well you know." James seemed at a loss for words.

"It was exciting. There were jugglers and tumblers,"

Sarah replied. "I even saw a dancing bear."

"Really?" James was fascinated as only a young boy would be. "Was he huge?"

"Not near as huge as you," Sarah laughed, "but, very ferocious." Sarah rummaged around in her bag and pulled out the wind chime she made for James. Jeffory helped her fashion it prior to leaving Tellishire. He had an old brush they took the bristles out of and sanded down for a nice round platform for the beads and copper to hang from. He helped her drill the holes for the jute with his awl.

"I made this for you," she said to James as she held it up in the firelight. It sparkled. The slight breeze that was not blocked by the bulk of the dragon's bodies stirred the chimes just enough to make them tinkle gently. "I bought the beads and the copper from a seller at the gathering. Uncle Jeffory helped me with the construction. I thought we could hang it outside the entrance to your cave."

"It's wonderful," James said. The pupils of his eyes were huge with hardly any color showing. He was so intently concentrating on the chimes, like a cat on an oblivious mouse.

"It really is lovely," Farloft added. "It reminds me of…"

I elbowed Sarah. "Get comfortable," I whispered. "I feel a story coming on."

17 FARLOFT AND THE WIZARD'S QUARREL

"She was beautiful," Farloft sighed, "with eyes as clear and bright in color as those blue glass beads," he indicated with a nod of his head toward the wind chime. "Her name was Belice and I loved her."

In all my years in Farloft's company he never confessed to having been in love. I pulled my cloak up around me and settled down anxious to hear this story.

"She surprised me the day we met. I was hunting. Her color so matched the blue sky around us that she seemed to materialize out of thin air." Farloft toyed with the tip of his claw in the dirt. His thoughts far, far away. "I had known other females, but none like her. She was a Norse dragon. Her eyes were just a few shades darker than her lovely iridescent blue body."

"What was she doing in Midland when she was a Norse dragon?" James asked. His father often told dragon stories around the fire at night when James was younger and human. He knew Norse dragons roamed the far north, not anywhere near Farloft's territory.

"It was just an accident," Farloft explained. "A wonderful accident. She was riding a high current and drifted south before she realized."

"Did you love her instantly?" Sarah asked, warming to the story. She was of an age to embrace romance be it human or dragon.

"Yes, it was love-at-first-sight," Farloft confessed. His voice took on a dreamy quality. "We traveled together for months - roaming the skies, playing in the clouds, drinking in the sunsets. We couldn't get enough of each other that summer." He paused as though lost in revelry.

I stirred the coals of the fire and tossed another branch on it. I didn't know whether I wanted to ask what happened or just wait to see if Farloft was going to elaborate.

Farloft finally picked up the thread of the story. "Winter came early that year. Rain and wind killed the crops before they could be harvested. Without the root crops and grain the people were forced to kill their livestock. The early rains were followed by heavy snowfall. Belice and I hunted for the humans that winter and into the spring. We ended up depleting the land of wildlife to keep the people alive. The snow stayed far into the spring making it difficult for the villagers to get their fields planted. That year was followed by yet another early, hard winter. There was no game in the area by then. Between the villagers, the castle staff and two dragons, we had hunted the kingdom until it was bare."

"It must have been like the year of the plague," James said, remembering how hungry he and the other villagers had been.

"Very much like that James," Farloft confirmed. "And the people were just as surly and unhappy then too. By the time the second year came around the people were beginning to turn against we dragons. We ate too much. We were the ones who stripped the land of the wildlife. There was no thought to the fact we gave much of it to the humans."

Farloft shook his head in dismay. "The real unrest began when someone saw Belice and I playing. We had resorted to catching fish. She was laughing at me trying to outmaneuver one in the stream. It was far to small to be something I could easily catch. Being a Norse Dragon she did not breathe smoke. Instead, her breath chilled. She breathed upon the stream, the water cooled, the fish slowed, and I was able to catch several without any further trouble."

"Why would that cause unrest?" Sarah asked. "Did the person who saw it want some of the fish?"

"No, child." Farloft inhaled and released the breath with a deep sigh. "The person spread the rumor that the bad weather, the rain, the snow, the long winters were all connected with Belice's arrival. That she was the cause of the people's suffering. She could breath on the land and turn it to ice. Therefore, it was her fault."

"Surely, people didn't believe that after all you did for them," Sarah countered.

"I am afraid they did," Farloft said. "The rumor was spread by a very reliable member of the human community. The people wanted someone to blame. They needed to vent their anger."

Farloft rose, backed up out from under the oak, and lifted his wings into a temple over his back in a big stretch. He walked out away from the fire and sat down with his back to us looking up at the stars. I did my own stretch, rose and went out to stand at his side.

"That must have only widened the rife between human and dragon in the kingdom," I said in a quiet voice at Farloft's side.

"The tip of the wing, as they say," Farloft acknowledged. "Later that winter while I was hunting further afield, still trying to fill all of our stomachs, dragon and human alike, hunters surprised Belice in the valley below our home and killed her. She was slow because she was carrying our child."

I placed my hand on Farloft's shoulder. "I am so sorry." I leaned into him and hugged his tree trunk sized leg. So much had happened since I was away.

"I did not make things any better by my actions. I came close to burning the village to the ground that day. It is not a day I like to remember. Not my finest hour," he admitted apologetically.

It dawned on me then. I was sure I had the answer. "It was Laval that spread the rumor," I said. It was not a question and Farloft did not deny it. He just leaned over and huffed gently into my hair.

18 UNDER THE SPELL OF THE ZONGULDAK RUBY

I spoke to the servants and the guards in the castle as I made my way down the corridor to Laval's quarters. Sarah reminded me when we returned yesterday from our trip that I promised to look in on the wizard. She noticed, and heard around the castle, that he was not himself - being very distracted and preoccupied. The potions he prepared were not having their usual effect. Many of his concoctions backfired and even caused minor damage to his patients. The talk heard whispered by many of the castle's occupants was he might have outlived his usefulness. This never would have been uttered about the King's wizard in the past. If nothing else, people would have been too frightened of the punishment if overheard by either the wizard or the king.

Laval's door was partially open when I arrived, so I knocked lightly and entered. There was a shuffling noise from the corner where he sat by the window. He jumped to his feet in surprise. His hand actually went for the dagger at his waist.

"What are you doing here?" He demanded.

"I'm sorry, Laval. I did not mean to startle you," I apologized. "I rode along with Sarah for her sitting with Prince William. I thought I might drop by and have a cup of tea with you while I was here."

He looked about as thought he lost something and then back at me. In an angry voice he said, "I don't have time to sit about drinking tea." Thinking better his voice softened a bit. "Perhaps another time," he said dismissively.

"Are you all right, Laval? You don't seem…" I faltered. "Is there anything I can do?"

"There is nothing the matter," he said in a more civil tone. "I am just busy. You'll excuse me. I must get back to work."

He had not been working. He was sitting when I arrived. Both his desk and his work bench were empty. I thought I heard something from behind him. It sounded like a voice singing softly. I cocked my head and asked, "What's that?"

"What's what?" Laval countered.

"That voice." I listened more carefully. I could hear the voice, but not the words, as though it were muffled. "Surely you hear it?"

"I cannot say that I do." Laval approached me and took my arm. He started to guide me toward the door. "I really must insist that you go, Theresa."

I could swear I knew that voice - that I had heard it before. I felt a cold chill lift the hair on the back of my neck. The voice grew stronger and I could tell now it was coming from the foot of the drapery by the chair the wizard was sitting in. I gave my arm a twist to release myself from his grasp and dove for the drape.

"Stop," he cried. "It's mine."

I came up with a wad of drapery in my hand, but something was tangled up in it. Whatever it was, it was singing loudly now. Laval grabbed at my hands as I came to my feet and it slipped out of my grasp, out of the drape and on to the floor. I could not believe my eyes. It was the Zonguldak Ruby. There was no doubt in my mind. Laval scooped it up and shoved it into the folds of his robe. No wonder he was acting so odd. The last time I saw the ruby was in Farloft's cave. Had Laval stolen it? Did he know what he had? Obviously not, or he would have rid himself of it and not be in this almost hypnotic state.

"Laval, you need to give me that." I held out my hand.

"No! It is mine." He backed away from me, stumbling over the footstool in the process.

I didn't want to go into how he got the thing. I just wanted to get it away from him. It was enchanted and only brought trouble wherever it was. He backed further away toward the door to his inner chamber.

"Wait," I raised my hand. He was under its spell. He would never willingly give it up. I decided to try a different approach. "You need to put it somewhere safe, Laval. Somewhere so no one can take it away from you. Do you have a hidden place, a fortified place where it can be locked away?" If there was enough metal between it and him, he wouldn't be able to hear it and the spell would be broken. More than that, he would realize he had been under a spell. How the hell did Laval get hold of the Zonguldak Ruby?

"Yes, someplace safe," he murmured. He grasp the hem of his cape and pulled it tightly about him. He muttered an incantation and promptly disappeared under a cloud of smoke.

I stood looking at an empty room. My next stop needed to be Farloft's.

19 CORONATIONS, NEW KINGS AND THE ZONGULDAK RUBY

My meeting with Farloft had to wait. I was called to the castle the next day to help attend to the King. He died peacefully yesterday, surrounded by family and friends.

William's public coronation will be next week.

Sarah and I are invited.

I doubt that Sarah will have his portrait completed in time.

*****

The coronation was splendid. Because I was at the former King's bedside prior to his death, and because Sarah is doing the new King's portrait, we were given a seat fairly close to the front of the church. William looked very much the part – dressed all in blue and shiny as a new button.

His sister Larkin walked stately in his wake. I know she was disappointed, being the eldest and yet unable to rule based on her sex. One day perhaps the kingdom will see that a man is not always the wise choice. I am reserving my opinion about William until he has been on the throne for a year at least. Perhaps everyone's worries are for naught. Perhaps he has been more observant then we think and will make a good king to his people.

After the ceremony, the King proceeded to the balcony to greet his subjects. Laval was at his side. The King waved. When the clapping and cheering settled down he stepped to the front of the balcony to address his people.

"We all know our land has seen hard times in the past few years. I hope to make this a turning point in our history. As a symbol of the good fortune in our future I wish to direct your eyes to the tower above," he raised his hand and pointed to the tallest turret. The point was covered with a large cloth that rippled in the morning breeze.

At that moment I noticed the guards standing behind us holding onto a rope attached to the cloth which trailed down off the turret.

"Our loyal and honored wizard, Laval, has given your ruler a gift which will be a symbol of bounty." The King nodded to the guards who drew the rope down revealing an object at the top of the tower. Tumbling in an invisible ball (no doubt fashioned by

Laval himself) the object threw off sparkling lights of red and gold. "I wish the Kingdom a most prosperous new beginning," the King shouted over the top of his people's cheers and whistles.

I cringed inside. It was the Zonguldak Ruby - the enchanted stone of disaster. Heaven help us all.

20 STUBBORN OLD DRAGON

"I never thought he would give it away," Farloft said defensively.

"Well he did," I almost shouted at the dragon. "And to the King! What were you thinking????" I paced back and forth outside Farloft's lair. "He's put it in some kind of a translucent spire at the top of the highest tower. Heaven only knows what it can do up there with all to see."

"It wasn't Farloft's fault," James said defensively. "I was the one who gave it to Laval."

"You may have been the one who gave it to him, but Farloft is the one who knew the havoc it could reap." I frowned at the older dragon. "He should have stopped you."

Farloft shook his head. "It seemed like a good idea at the time."

"It certainly did," James chimed in with a smile.

"Well, it wasn't," I chastised the two. "What are we going to do? The King inadvertently wished on it."

"But, you said he wished for prosperity for the kingdom," James said.

"Did you bother to tell James about the Ruby before he gave it away?" I asked Farloft. "Anything that is wished in the presence of that stone becomes twisted and perverted."

"You don't understand," Farloft replied gruffly. "It seemed appropriate at the time."

I could see I was not going to get any further with the dragons as far as determining why Laval had the ruby in the first place. In any case, it was the immediate problem I came up here to resolve. Just because the King wished for prosperity did not guarantee that was what was going to occur. In fact, making a wish like that in the presence of the Zonguldak Ruby almost assured the opposite would happen.

"Can you fly in tonight and grab it from the tower?" I asked. We needed to get the ruby back in Farloft's cave where it could do no more harm.

"It is against the code," Farloft huffed in an offended voice. The dragon code is very lengthy and I do not claim I know even half of it. It is very convoluted in spots, but I do know dragons must live honestly. Stealing the ruby would technically be against the code.

I tried a bit of logic. "It wouldn't be stealing, Farloft. You would only be taking back what you gave in the first place."

"Well…"

I rushed on. "And, since it is for the good of the recipient, I think an exception could be made. Don't you?"

"Perhaps," Farloft said deep in thought. "However, I did not technically give the ruby to Laval. It was James. So perhaps under the circumstance, as you say, it would be permissible for James to retrieve it."

"James, do you think you could fly to the castle tonight and get the ruby from the tower," I asked.

"However," Farloft interrupted. He hesitated a moment in thought, then went on. "I cannot allow James to go to the castle. It is extremely dangerous so close to humans. He doesn't fly well enough yet."

"But Farloft, we have to retrieve it before the King voices anymore of his desires," I argued. "And, we have never seen the ruby so prominently displayed. Neither you nor I know what will happen now that it is not concealed and kept secret by just the owner. What happens if it begins to act on anyone's wishes who gaze on it?" It was a thought too horrible to conceive.

"James cannot go," Farloft repeated. "I must remain firm on this point. I will not allow him to go into certain danger so close to humans."

"Then you have to go get it," I was almost to the shouting stage I was so frustrated.

"As I have explained, the code prevents me from retrieving the stone."

Damn the dragon's code. "Then I guess I will have to do it myself," I stated flatly. "Thank you so very much for your help." Damn stubborn old dragon. I turned and marched back toward my horse.

"Healer?" Farloft called to my receding back. "I wouldn't try that. Laval has most likely put some sort of protective spell on it. You might find yourself turned into a chicken, or a goat, or worse."

"Thanks for the warning," I shot back, as I pulled myself up on Knicker for the long ride home.

21 THE CURSE OF THE ZONGULDAK RUBY

"Damn stubborn dragons," I said yet again, as I paced the floor of the cottage. Sarah was beside herself trying to calm me down.

"Maybe it won't be as bad as you think," she offered.

I rolled my eyes at her. She had no idea. "It has only just started, Sarah. I am afraid it will snowball from here on."

I was unable to procure the Zonguldak Ruby from the tower two days ago. The chance of being turned into a chicken or a goat was beside the point, the new King stationed a guard at the bottom of the stairs up into the tower – no one was allowed pass him. But, that was not what had me fired up.

Within twenty-four hours of the coronation, a sinister group appeared to infiltrate the kingdom's borders. It started as a trickle, but now was a steady stream of the lawless and homeless of the country. They were stealing from the already depleted stores of the poor. They looted homes left without owners after the plague swept the land. For these few, 'the

Kingdom was prosperous,' as the King wished in his speech. However, I'm sure it was not what the King had in mind.

But, that was not the end of it. You could hear the ruby singing throughout the castle and into the edges of the closest village. I feared its influence had spread as I warned Farloft it might.

Earlier in the day, today, I was called to act as midwife. Annah was having her second child. I scooted out her husband and their first child, Adam, a lovely, active child of five or so. He was so full of questions about the prospects of a new sibling I literally had to close the door in his face in order to get rid of him and get on with my duties.

It was an easy delivery. The little girl looked healthy in every aspect. Unfortunately though, the child was born mute. She made the act of crying, but not a sound escaped her tiny, pink lips.

Annah hugged her close as tears ran down her cheeks. "I did this. I asked the Lord to give me a quieter child, a peaceful child. Adam is so full of energy. I just didn't think I could keep up with two. I had no idea God would take me so literally."

God did not take her literally. I was as sure as a hunting dog on a fresh scent that it was the

Zonguldak Ruby that did the deed.

*****

I put my hands over my ears. "I can hear the damn thing singing clear out here," I complained.

Sarah approached me cautiously and drew my hands down. "It's just that you are sensitive to it. I can't hear it until I am almost within the castle walls."

"Be very careful what you say in its presence," I warned. "I fear it is feeding off everyone's desires." I grabbed my cloak off the hook by the door. "I have to see Farloft and get him to change his mind."

Sarah took my cloak from me. "Not tonight. It's late and you have had a rough day. You need to rest." She pushed me gently into a chair and handed me a mug of tea. "Drink," she ordered. "I'll fix us some dinner and after a good night's rest, you can go argue with Farloft as much as you like and I promise I won't interfere." She drizzled a spoon of honey in my mug.

I was tired. I am not as young as I think I am in my head. I took a sip of the tea. It felt good all the way down. Sarah bustled about frying up bacon at the hearth, slicing the early tomatoes and fresh bread into thick slices. The aroma made my mouth water. I hadn't eaten since earlier this morning. No time for lunch when a baby is waiting to be born. That brought my thoughts back to Annah and her child. How many other good intentioned wishes were going to go awry before I could convince that stubborn dragon to see reason?

22 POTATO VINES GONE WILD

Micah and I stood staring at his potato vines. The vines had overwhelmed his tool shed and brought the flimsy building to its knees, now they were headed for his cottage – not a good prospect considering it was built about as sturdy as the shed.

"I hacked at 'em 'til dare nothin' but stumps and dare back again the next day. Ain't never seen anythin' like it in my life," he said scratching his head. "No tubers, just bush." He illustrated his point by pitch forking at the base of one of the vines, nothing but roots, no potatoes.

"I thought you bein' a wise woman, might have a thought on what to do," he said.

My thoughts were not for gentle minded folk. I wanted to throttle one very old dragon. This was another example of the ruby's doing, I was sure.

"We all been hopin' and prayin' our crops 'ould be better this yar, but I don't need vine, I need the tubers," he lamented.

This was the third unusual occurrence I had been

brought out to in the last two days. I didn't know what to tell Micah. I couldn't tell him the ruby did it. If I did, the word would spread and there would be a revolt against the new King for sure. They would never trust him again. And, nothing I had done so far made an impression on anyone important enough to take the ruby down and dispose of it.

I convinced Sarah to talk to King William about the ruby, but he has been bewitched by it. He can't see the connection between the stone and the unusual happenings in his kingdom.

I spoke with Farloft again to no avail. He will not budge on letting James retrieve the stone. If anything, he is even more adamant since the lower class thieves and hooligans have moved into the area. There has been a bounty on dragons for years.

I had another audience with Laval and begged him to give the ruby back to Farloft. He would not hear of it. He is sure the stone will bring the Kingdom prosperity. When I pointed out the lawless element that has moved in, he just shook his head and said it was a sign of the times. Once the Kingdom recovered from the after affects of the plague, they would move on.

They are all blind to the stones influence. I can hear

it singing now all the way to the river crossing. It is feeding on the people's wishes and dreams, and in the process perverting them into nightmares.

23 THE ATTACK

I heard them before I saw them coming. It was James, thrown a bit off balance by the fact that he was carrying Sarah. He had his right leg crooked up for her to sit on and she had her arms wrapped tightly about his neck. She was sobbing when he hit the ground in front of the cottage. She gave him a quick squeeze and ran past me into the house.

I looked from the door back to James. "What happened?"

"I heard shouting," James started to explain. "Three men had her pinned down in a ditch. She was chucking rocks at them, but before I could reach her they got to her. They ran when they saw me coming, but they took Tolly and all her art stuff. "

"Did you recognize the men?"

"No. They were from that new rough crowd that has moved in," James replied. "I'm going back after Tolly. He'll answer me if I call. I'll find him and give those guys what's coming to them." The young dragon turned a deep crimson color as he talked about revenge. His head spikes rose like a dog's hackles. I could feel the heat radiating off his skin as his dragon's fire built. He spread his wings and started to take flight.

I reached out and laid my hand on his snout. "Calm down, James. I don't want you getting hurt and neither would Sarah. I have to go into her now. Please promise me you will stay here until we determine the proper course of action to take."

"What about Tolly?" James had become close to Sarah's horse in the past few months. He and Tolly could actually communicate in a limited way.

"I don't think they will hurt her, James. She is worth money to them." I reached out and patted him on his shoulder. "You'll be able to track her down later. I need you to stay here for now. Promise me?"

He hung his head and mumbled "I promise."

"Good. Now go hide over there in the edge of the woods until I call you." I didn't wait for him to move. I headed in to see to Sarah.

24 JAMES TAKES ACTION

Sarah was curled up in a knot on her bed. Her sobs had subsided to sniffles.

I sat on the edge of the bed at her back. "Are you hurt, Sarah?" I asked softly.

She turned over and snuggled her head into my lap. "No. I was just very scared. I don't know what would have happened if James hadn't come along."

I picked a leaf out of her hair and soothed it back. The shoulder of her dress was torn. She was muddy from her scuffle. I could reach the water bucket we kept on the hearth for washing up from my place on her bed. I leaned over and dunked the end of the towel in the water. I tilted up her face to have a look. Her lip was bruised with dried blood on it. One of them had hit her.

"Let's get you cleaned up and some salve on that cut." I felt like James – I was having a hard time controlling my temper. However, my temper was not as focused as James'. I couldn't decide if I blamed Farloft, Laval, King William, or the hoodlums for what happened to Sarah. In my mind they were all guilty.

Sarah cleaned up and changed her dress. I put salve on her lip, the palms of her hands and her knees, which had been skinned in the tussle. I was brushing her hair while she was sipping a warm cup of broth when I remembered I left James waiting.

"I totally forgot about James." I jumped to my feet. "I told him to wait in the woods. I should have told him you were going to be all right ages ago." It had gotten dark out. I grabbed my cloak off the hook by the door. "I'll only be gone a few minutes," I assured Sarah. "I'll be right back."

"Wait," Sarah called. "I want to go with you and thank him properly." She swung her cloak about her shoulders and we headed out to see James.

But, James wasn't there. I hoped he just got tired of waiting, but I knew how much he cared about Sarah, so my heart told me his leaving was not a case of just going home. My fears were confirmed when we turned to see Tolly trotting into the yard with neither a rider, nor a dragon in tow.

25 FARLOFT FLIGHT

Farloft landed in front of the cottage just as I was mounting Knicker to go look for James.

"Have you seen James?" Farloft asked before he even folded his wings.

"I was just going to look for him. He rescued Sarah from three hoodlums this afternoon and I told him to wait for me until I looked to Sarah. When we came out, he was gone." I explained. "I am worried, Farloft. He was very upset about Sarah and the fact that the men had taken Tolly. I thought I talked him out of going after them."

Farloft looked at Sarah holding Tolly's reins. "But, Tolly is here."

"He came home alone about a half hour ago."

"Stay here," he said. "I'll go look for him."

Farloft was gone before either of us could object.

26 KING WILLIAM SEEKS THE RUBY

Waiting is the hardest task. Sarah and I didn't hear anything from Farloft throughout the night. We tried to sleep, but ended up napping off and on in our chairs by the fire instead.

King William, Laval and a score of heavily armed knights arrived the next day at our door. It was very early morning. It was as if the King had announced yesterday, "We ride at sunrise." And, they had - straight to our door.

"We are seeking the dragon, Farloft," William informed us upon pulling up his horse in front of the cottage. He didn't even dismount.

"And good morning to you too," I corrected. Frankly some folk might have been scared to correct the King, but I had known him since birth and actually changed his diapers numerous times.

"Good morning, Healer, Sarah." He nodded grudgingly at first me and then Sarah. "Can you direct us to the dragon's lair?"

I wasn't about to tell them where to find Farloft and James. Obviously, Laval, sitting at the King's side, had chosen to stay quiet about the location of their home, he knew as well as I did where it was located.

"I am sorry, your highness. I cannot help you." I put my arm around Sarah in a silent effort to communicate to her she had to stand with me on this one, even if she did like William. "I do not know the location of the lair. Farloft and I often talk, but it is in the forest or on the road. May I ask why you wish to speak to him with armed knights at your side."

"He has stolen what is mine," William stated gruffly. "He ripped the ruby Laval gave me from the tower, along with half the roof of the turret."

How could I have missed its disappearance? I realized I could no longer hear the song of the stone. But, it was not Farloft, I thought. It had to be James' doing. Farloft wouldn't have made the mistake of taking part of the roof. He would have just fetched the jewel.

"I believe you are mistaken, your highness," I gently corrected. "You know my views on the removal of the stone. I spoke with Farloft on the same subject and he assured me it was against the Dragon Code for him to remove the stone from someone he did not give it to. He told me it had to be willingly given back to him in order for him to shield its power in his cave." I caught an odd expression on Laval's face. Was it disappointment or anticipation? Whatever it was, it was fleeting. His face returned to the stone expression of someone who knows he is being watched.

How long would the influence of the ruby linger over the King? Farloft would know. I desperately wanted to talk to him. Where were the dragons? Farloft would have come back if he found James. Wouldn't he?

"He obviously lied to you." William pulled hard on his reins. "We will find him without your help, but believe me I will remember this lack of cooperation with your liege."

The group galloped off in the general direction of Farloft's cave.

"Someone should have given that boy a licking when he was younger," I mumbled under my breath.

27 STING OF THE RUBY'S CURSE

Farloft must have been watching the cottage, because King William and his entourage had just disappeared into the woods when Farloft landed noiselessly in front of the cottage. Sarah and I hadn't even made it back inside.

"I need you ladies to come with me," he said without preamble.

"Is it James? Is he all right?" Sarah asked.

"Yes and no," Farloft answered. "I found him, but it took me most of the night to get him home."

"Is he hurt?" I asked.

"You will have to see," Farloft responded with a weary look.

"Sarah, fetch our cloaks and bring my bag, please. I will saddle the horses." Sarah headed for the door at a run.

"No horses," Farloft said. "I will take you both. We need to get back to him quickly."

"Sarah, you had best change into some of my britches," I advised. "Farloft's scales will chafe you legs otherwise."

"I'll only be a minute." She ran into the cottage.

"King William was here. I imagine you saw," I said to Farloft once Sarah was out of hearing range. "He believes you stole the ruby, but it was James, wasn't it?"

"Yes, but would it were I who tried for the stone," Farloft said with a tone of regret. I thought I saw a tear gather in his eye.

"What happened?" I dreaded the answer.

"James first went to retrieve Tolly. He was angry, but he did no more damage than singe some hair. His mere presence sent them running. Tolly bucked so hard they left her behind. James sent her home and went on to get the ruby." Farloft paused for a breath. "Oh Theresa," he said and a tear did fall from his eye.

"Just tell me, Farloft." The suspense was more than I could handle. James couldn't be dead - or could he?

"He succeeded in grabbing the ruby and he made it to the ocean and dropped it in before Laval's spell took effect. It must have been triggered by the release of the ruby. He is lucky he didn't drown."

"Drown?"

"The spell turned his wings to iron. He can't fly. He can't even move." Farloft lifted his head and let out a burst of dragon fire. "I am going to kill Laval," he swore.

"Oh no!" Sarah cried behind me. I don't know what she was exclaiming about, James plight or Farloft's declaration. Both were equally disastrous.

28 GROUNDED DRAGON

"Don't struggle, James," I cautioned. He was lying on the flat area just outside the cave entrance. From the moment we landed and slid from Farloft's back he had been trying to rise to his feet. His body and face were blood red from his anger and frustration. Unlike his body, his wings were coal black and solid iron, heavy, useless appendages that had him pinned helplessly to the ground. Even holding his head up was an effort.

"Easy," Sarah said. She stroked the hot skin of his neck. "Do as Aunt T says. You need to save your strength until she figures out what we have to do."

James relaxed a bit under Sarah's hand. He leaned into her shoulder as she knelt at his side and big tears ran down the sides of his face. "Don't worry, James. We're here now. Aunt T will think of something."

I got up to fetch some water from the pool at the front of the cave. I slipped a light dose of sleeping powder in it and brought it back in my hat. I handed it to Sarah. "Here, hold this for him to drink and then fetch him another when he finishes that." I instructed gently. Sarah nodded and took the hat.

I walked over to where Farloft stood a distance away. His anger also generated heat. It was like standing next to a bonfire. "Can you do anything?" he asked without taking his eyes off James.

"I don't think so," I admitted. "Without knowing what Laval did exactly, I don't think I can reverse it."

"It was meant for me," Farloft said with a snarl. "I should have listened to you, Healer. I was headstrong and stupid."

"Well, I will not argue with you on those counts, but hindsight will do us no good now." I was so sorry what I thought was going wrong had so terribly come to pass. "I did notice Laval was not volunteering to bring the King here. He acted like he didn't know where your lair was located."

"He wants something." Farloft's tail slashed across the ground flinging rocks in his pent up rage. "As soon as he rids himself of the King's presence, he will come here to bargain and I will be ready."

29 LAVAL'S CURSE

Farloft was right. Laval arrived by himself the next morning.

"You are lucky I don't roast you where you stand," Farloft spat. His dragon fire smoldered just below the surface causing his nose to puff smoke with each word.

"If you do," Laval stated confidently "you will never see James fly again."

They were at a stalemate. Laval already confirmed Farloft's theory that the spell for the lead wings was meant for him. Laval hoped to ground the dragon and let the King's men deal with his killing. However, James took the ruby instead. Therefore, the spell fell on him. Now Laval changed his tactic. He shifted from killer to blackmailer without hesitation.

"If you promise to take James and leave this kingdom forever, I will reverse the spell on James and you can both fly away," Laval offered.

"This is my home!" Farloft shouted.

"Then spend your life taking care of a flightless dragon and watch him die despondent and angry at you for leaving him trapped on the ground," Laval yelled back.

"I would never be angry at you," James countered. "It's him I hate!" He spat fire at Laval, but because of his inability to move, he missed and hit the bush beside him instead. The bush burst into flame and sprinkled burning embers onto Laval's cloak. He jumped to one side and shook them off.

"Best control your protege, Farloft. You wouldn't want him to take the decision out of your hands."

Farloft went to James' side and nuzzled him as he lay pinned to the ground. "James, please, let me handle this."

"You can't leave here," James sobbed. "This has been your home for over a thousand years. Where would you go? Dragon's are hated everywhere. At least here you are safe."

"WE are safe," Farloft corrected. "My life would be pointless without you to share it with me." Farloft had moved past his anger and was thinking. "We could go east. They still honor the dragon there, don't they Theresa?"

"Yes." I did not want to comment further. I would miss Farloft terribly if he left. I would much rather see Laval gone. Perhaps there was a way. "Sarah, I want you to go get King William."

"No!" Laval shouted. "This is none of his business."

I placed my hands on my hips and stared at the wizard. "The kingdom and what happens in it is his business." I could almost bet the reason Laval had been able to leave the King's side was that the King no longer sought the Ruby. Its effects had diminished enough he lost interest and went home. I also hoped with that loss of interest, he had come to his senses and was able to see the damage it had done and would see the correct person to blame in this whole fiasco.

30 KING WILLIAM'S ARRIVAL

It took all of that day and most of the night for Sarah to fetch King William to Farloft's lair.

Farloft and I built a fire. Not that he or James needed any warmth, but I could use some heat for my bones. When Laval started to sidle up to the blaze, Farloft thumped his tail forcefully enough to shake the earth between the fire and the wizard and ordered him away. Laval moved off to a safe distance and made his own small fire. He was huddled there now. No doubt scheming further – devising plots against dragon and king.

When the King arrived Laval rushed to his side before he could even dismount. "Your Highness, I have downed the dragons, they are yours to slay," He announced with pride and a wave of his hand in our direction. "I am afraid the smaller one dropped your precious ruby in the ocean, but I am sure there is much more treasure for the taking in the lair, once you have slain the dragons."

William dismounted and Sarah took him by the

hand. He acted as if he were sleepwalking as Sarah led him to the fire.

"He has been this way since I found him in the chapel at the castle. His guard forbade me to take him, but I sneaked him out."

Farloft rose to his full height and looked down into the valley below. "They followed you."

I looked over the edge of the cliff and saw the torches of the band of guards following Sarah's trail. If each had a torch there must be a dozen men. If not, there were more, many more.

31 SPELLS, CURSES AND HIDDEN AGENDAS

It started with Farloft trying to help the King regain his consciousness and deteriorated into a physical scuffle between Laval and me. Laval tried to interfere when Farloft began to draw the King's attention to his own eyes. Laval accused him of hypnotizing the King, which he wasn't. Dragons can see deep into the souls of men. Deep enough to find what is truly there.

When Laval stepped forward with his staff in hand leveled at Farloft, I was close enough to grab it. Now we were on the ground wrestling for control of the staff which was shooting out sprays of bright energy. It felt like holding on to a bolt of lightning. Every joint in my body was singing.

We rolled to the edge of the cliff and I heard Sarah cry out. Farloft's paw appeared between us and the edge, impeding our emanate roll off the edge. Farloft made a grab for Laval, but missed as I rolled over on top of the wizard.

It was at this point that King William's troops arrived. Captain Haben was not a man of indecision. He was a well trained and seasoned officer nearly as old as the former King. He immediately dispatched his men to separate us as we continued to roll away from the dragons and toward his men. Strong arms yanked me to my feet and away from Laval. The staff went clattering to the ground as other hands brought the wizard to his feet.

"You will return the King to us immediately," the Captain ordered Farloft.

"I will not," Farloft replied. "The King is under a spell which must be removed before any more damage is done."

Captain Haben could see he and his men were at a disadvantage to try and force the dragon to return the King. He was about to order his men to release Laval, perhaps to help, when I struggled for my freedom and won. I spoke to the Captain very plainly.

"Captain, you know me. I delivered your daughter's baby. The silent one." As if I needed to remind him that the child was born mute. "That and many other odd happenings have been plaguing our kingdom over the past months. Those events were brought on by the Wizard and his gift to the King of the Zonguldak Ruby that was placed on the tower during the coronation. The Ruby was bewitched and could only bring disaster to those who heard its song."

Haben was not silencing me. Perhaps he heard it singing. I know there was talk of his daughter's child in the village. There were whispers about the other odd events in the area. Many people speculated on the hoodlums that arrived from nowhere to enter the kingdom causing mayhem and destruction.

"Haben, you can trust me," I said. "There need be no bloodshed here tonight. Farloft is old and wise. He can cure the King if you let him and then all will be revealed."

"Don't listen to her," Laval cried. "She is a witch herself. She probably put a spell on your daughter that caused the child to be mute."

"You know that is not true," Sarah said. She rushed over and stood beside me. "You, Thomas," she pointed at one of the soldiers. "Aunt T helped your mother get over her gout. Do you remember what pain she was in before the Healer administered to her? And you, Nathaniel," she pointed to another. "Your boy would have died this spring had it not been for the Healer. Who among you have not been touched by her healing?"

They all looked thoughtful including the Captain.

"Can't you see what they are doing?" Laval shouted. The soldier's grip had lessened on his arms and he made a lung for his staff. He picked it up on the run, dodging hands that reached to stop him. He was headed for the remaining group by the fire, Farloft, James and the King.

He took the path that was open, the area closest to the cliff's edge. His staff glowed in his hand as he cleared the people that could stop him. He raised it, but in his haste he tripped and the bolt from its end would have killed the King if Farloft had not succeeded in pushing William to safety behind one of James' iron wings.

Farloft let out a burst of dragon fire so intense we all had to turn and shield ourselves from its heat. When we turned back Laval was gone. Only his smoldering staff remained on the ground marking where he had been.

We all stood as though transfixed like the King - lost in our own thoughts. Farloft nuzzled the King from his hiding place. Sarah ran to William and James to make sure they were all right.

"We need to release King William from what I think is a spell Laval must have cast," I told Captain Haben and his men.

Haben nodded. I went to the King, picking up Laval's staff on the way.

32 A KINGLY SPELL

Captain Haben was old enough he had heard the stories from his grandfather, who also served the King of his time, about the dragon's joining forces with the inhabitants of the kingdom to defeat their enemies. He never fought or feared a dragon. He admired Farloft from a distance. After Farloft explained he intended to bring the King back from wherever he was lost in his mind, Haben told his soldiers to put their weapons away and relax. We all sat in a semicircle around Farloft, James and the King.

Farloft balanced William between his two front paws. The King and the dragon made eye contact and it was as if neither could look away. Farloft's eyes changed color slowly from their pure gold to a deep amber. The King's expression, which was originally quite vacant, turned to more of a questioning look. Slowly his brow knit and his hands reached out to grip Farloft's paws. Not a word passed between them, but you could feel multitudes being said in their eyes. The King jerked violently once, which brought Haben to his feet, but William calmed quickly and I was able to pull the Captain back down to his place by me.

The King's expressions ran the gauntlet. They went from surprised to contrite – smiles to crying. Finally there was only wonder in his face as Farloft broke eye contact and let the King settle into a sleeping position with his head in Sarah's lap. "He will be back to himself when he awakes."

Haben covered William with his cloak and threw a few more branches on the fire. "You men set up camp. We will spend what is left of the night here until the King is fit to travel."

Most of the men just wrapped their cloaks around them and settled down where they had been sitting.

I settled Sarah with her back to James and leaned over the King. I brushed his hair from his brow. "Will things be better when he awakes?" I asked, as I turned to Farloft.

"I gave him a glimpse of his kingdom's history in hope it would make him a better King." Farloft curled his tail around him and laid his head on his paws. "But, I got a glimpse of his soul in the process. It did nothing to calm my fears."

I drew in a deep breath that came out in a hard sigh. I had hoped...

I turned to James already fast asleep with his head curled as close to Sarah as he could reach without being able to change position. "Tomorrow, we work on your problem, dear." I patted him gently on the snout and took my own position by the fire with my back to Farloft's side.

33 THE SEARCH FOR THE CURE

I was standing by Captain Haben as he saddled his horse for me when I overheard Sarah and King William in hushed conversation.

"I need to stay with James. He's young and frightened," Sarah was explaining.

"He has Farloft and I am leaving Haben here too," William countered. It had already been decided that I would ride the Captain's steed back to the castle to see if we could find the remedy for James' wings. William had chosen Haben to remain because he had the greatest respect for the dragons. The King felt that there would be less of a chance for misunderstanding between Farloft and Haben than one of the younger, less experienced men. "I really would like you to ride with us. I have many thoughts running through my head. I want to talk to you about all of it."

"We will have plenty of time to talk later, William. Discuss your thoughts with Aunt T. She has a very sound mind. I think you will find her input invaluable." She patted his arm affectionately. "After all, we don't have another extra horse. Stop by the cottage on the way back and pick up Tolly, will you? We'll talk on the way home after all of this is settled." Sarah was so positive that we would find a cure for James and so certain that William would come back to retrieve her. Ah…how sweet is young love.

*****

"Has he ever done that to you before?" William asked. We had been riding hard since early this morning, but had slowed to give the horses a breather.

"No, he hasn't, but from what you tell me perhaps I will ask him to someday. It sounds to me as though it gave you a unique look at our past." I stood up in my stirrups to give my seat a rest. I was not used to riding hard and certainly not in a rough military saddle such as Haben's.

"It was truly enlightening. Had it not been for Laval's treachery over the years, the dragons would never have fallen from favor. They were so instrumental in assisting the Kingdom in the past. Those hoodlums that moved in this past few months never would have risk coming within miles of our borders back when the dragons rode the wind in our skies."

It seemed William had learned the advantage of having dragons in the kingdom.

"Perhaps in time you and Farloft will become friends." I could think of nothing better for the kingdom's future. Farloft would make an excellent adviser. I had been using him as one on and off throughout my life.

"You know if you had said that twenty-four hours ago, I would have denied it for all my worth, but now I think it is a possibility."

"I have no doubt that Farloft would be pleased to meet you halfway in any attempt you would make to be friends. He is a stubborn dragon, but not a stupid one. He will see the advantages that can be had from forming an alliance with your highness."

"I certainly hope so," Williams said, as he spurred his horse back into a gallop.

34 DOVES AND SPELLS

It was way too obvious. Not only did Laval leave his journal of spells open to the page for the protective sphere, but he noted, in his own hand, the reversal spell. It had to be a trap. The wizard was reaching beyond the grave to cause further chaos.

"I need to test this," I said reluctantly. I assumed I would use the staff to focus the spell. "Stand back," I warned and motioned everyone away from the table in the center of the room. I cleared a space on the surface, pointed the staff toward it and uttered the incantation. I have some experience in casing spells so I was not surprised when a small sphere appeared.

"Theresa, you are marvelous!" King William shouted. "I had no idea you were a conjurer."

"That's because I don't consider myself one. I am first and foremost a Healer." Now that I had created a sphere similar to the one that had contained the ruby, I had to find a way to test it. I walked to the cage of pet doves in the corner of the room and removed one. I brought it over and let it settle on the sphere. We all held out breath and watched. The bird stood for a moment on the sphere and then hopped down to the table's surface. We all stared in amazement as the dove's pale wings took on a darker shade and began to droop. It sat huddled and despondent on the table top with wings of iron. I gently stroked its head. "I'm sorry," I told it. "Let's get you back to right again."

I moved the offending sphere with the tip of the staff to the furthest edge of the table. I had no idea how far its influence would carry on the dove. I lowered the staff, touched the dove's wings where they overlapped in the back at the tail and pronounced the hand written phrase. Nothing happened.

"William will you hold the dove for a moment? I need to get rid of the sphere. It may be its presence that keeps the wings from returning to normal."

The King picked up the dove and withdrew to the far corner of the room. I used a spell of my own to destroy the sphere. The sphere was pulverized to dust.

With a nod from me, William returned the dove to the table. I touched the dove's wings and once again spoke the incantation. Nothing happened.

I went back to the journal to read further. William picked up the pitifully helpless dove again. He stroked it and carried it around with him as he walked the room thinking and waiting for me to do something.

"Sarah will be heartbroken if we cannot find a cure for James' plight, to say nothing of Farloft," I muttered to myself. "I just don't understand. It's a trick of some sort. This is the one time I wish I had known Laval better." I flipped through pages, but could find nothing further to assist me. I had created more pain rather than lessening it. I felt horrible about the dove. I had to find a solution. It was here. I just wasn't looking with the right eyes.

What luck that the King was thinking so hard about the problem at hand that he placed the dove on the wide window's ledge for a moment as he contemplated our problem further.

A wild dove came to see the creature that looked like a dove, but wasn't any longer. It cooed and brought our attention to the windowsill. Before the King could think to intercede, the wild dove had pushed the dove with the iron wings off the sill and out the window. We both ran to the window, but there was nothing to see. To my relief, the iron winged dove was not laying on the roof below, broken and dead. There was no sign of the dove. However, there were two normal doves cooing and cuddling on the adjacent tower's roof.

I strained my eyes to see the roof below. "Do you see the iron winged dove?" I asked anxiously.

"No, only those two over there," William pointed to the loving pair in amazement. He was coming to the same conclusion I had.

"Do you think we are missing the dove with the spell? Could it have slipped off the roof and down to the courtyard?"

"I don't think so. The roof is slanted the wrong way," William answered. He turned from looking at the pair of doves to look at me. "Do you think that is the dove?"

"Laval was very clever. He said the spell was meant for Farloft. The wizard would know Farloft would never think to break the spell by jumping off a cliff with iron wings."

I smiled with satisfaction. "But, Farloft could get James high enough to drop him."

"Let's try another dove just to make sure." I was not

afraid of killing the dove. Not now. I was sure we had found the way to break the spell. But, how would I ever convince Farloft to trust me enough to drop James.

35 CHANCES MUST BE TAKEN

We rode back to the dragon's lair as quickly as our mounts would allow, with only a short stop at the cottage to pick up Knicker and Tolly. The King insisted on accompanying me, but we left his guard at the castle. I had tested my theory on another four doves with success. Our arrival had been brought to the King's sister's attention when she saw the doves plummeting past her window with iron wings intact. She insisted on an explanation and the King was anxious to tell her of all that had happened. Larkin fed us while we recounted the events that had brought us to tossing mutated doves out the windows. She had a cook pack some supplies in a saddle bag for us. With fresh steeds we were on our way.

It was a new moon and dark as pitch. The last leg of the journey we climbed the mountain leading our horses for fear of a broken leg, ours or theirs.

Haben, Sarah, James and Farloft were clustered around a bonfire. Farloft was very animated, telling a story to keep all their minds off the process of waiting for us.

"Good evening, friends," Farloft greeted us as he rose to his feet.

Haben stood and offered the King his place on a cloak by the fire. I noticed it was Sarah's. I could see she didn't have any need of it. James was still red with frustration and anger, and no doubt warm, against her back. She sat up by his shoulder with his iron wing blocking what little breeze there was.

"And it is a good evening," I said. I stood before the fire warming my hands so I could see everyone in our little group. "I have good news, the King and I have found out how to reverse the spell."

"Do it! Do it now!" James almost shouted. He struggled beneath the weight of his iron wings.

Sarah rose and went to his head. She took his muzzle between her hands. "Stop it, James. You'll hurt yourself."

"We can't do it tonight," I started to explain. "We need daylight." It was then that I told them about the doves and what needed to be done to reverse James back to his old self.

"Based on our observations, distance, size of the doves and the time it took them to change back, we think you will have to carry James at least the height of this cliff higher before you drop him," William said.

"Drop him?" Farloft huffed and shook his head. "What happens if you are wrong in your calculations? James would not survive a fall from that height, not with iron wings to weigh him down."

"We have to take the chance, Farloft," James insisted. "I am willing. I can't live like this." He tried to shrug, but it didn't get past his neck. He just couldn't lift his wings off the ground.

"He's right Farloft," Sarah agreed. "You have to try. Perhaps you could take him higher for safeties sake - unless he's too heavy for you." Sarah's comment reached out and tweaked Farloft's ego just as she had intended it to.

"Of course I can lift him higher. I only want to be sure," Farloft countered gruffly.

"Then we'll do it tomorrow," James said.

"I am still not sure that is wise," the older dragon cautioned.

"We either do it tomorrow or I see if it will work from the height of this cliff," James threatened.

Farloft looked at me. "I know it will work," I said with conviction.

Farloft resigned himself. "Then we do it tomorrow."

36 FREE FALL

"Don't worry, James." I patted him on the muzzle. "I know it will work." I turned to Farloft. "He will fall for at least half the distance to the ground before his wings change," I warned.

"I intend to follow him down," Farloft stated flatly.

"Just don't grab him. I am not sure if the reversal attempt can be made again. Laval's spells were full of trickery. It would be just like him to put in a one-time-only reversal." I backed away from the two dragons as Farloft got a firm hold on his young friend.

Sarah rushed up and threw her arms around James' neck. "I'll see you when you land here, wings intact." She gave him a kiss on the nose for encouragement and then stepped quickly away.

"Let's get this done," Farloft said. "Ready, James?"

"Ready," James piped up.

Farloft spread his huge wings and took to the air

with James firmly placed in his large paws. His beats were strong and smooth as they rose higher and higher in the sky. Meer air currents could not lift the intense weigh of the two dragons.

"How high does he intend to take James," the King asked as we all gazed at the diminishing figures of Farloft and his burden.

"As high as he can. I suppose." It was not that Farloft did not trust me. He just wanted to be sure. Absolutely sure James would make it.

Sarah shielded her eyes from the sun. "There he goes," she said almost in a whisper.

All of us held our breath as we watched James plummet toward earth. Visions of my first encounter with James during his early flying lessons came rushing back, but this time Farloft had tucked his wings and was falling right beside James.

It was fast, so fast. Before we knew it they were at the rim of the cliff and still falling. We all rushed to the edge and watched them continue to fall.

I saw Farloft snap his wings open and reach for James, still careening earthward in his lead wings. Farloft misjudged the rate James was falling and he missed catching James by what looked like the width of my hand. Sarah screamed.

"No!" Sarah hollered.

Then it happened. James' wings popped open and he swooped up in a lazy curve gliding pass Farloft who was right on his tail trying to catch his laden body before he struck the ground.

"Catch me if you can," James taunted gleefully.

Farloft gave one mighty thrust of his wings downward and came to a screeching halt mid-air. Two more mighty beats and he had caught up to James.

The two landed on the cliff to the joy and cheers of the few humans who had been witness to the remarkable event. It would be one that would be told around hearths and campfires long into the future in this kingdom of the last dragons.

37 A ROYAL APPOINTMENT?

We made our way slowly and joyfully home. Farloft walked at the King's side aboard his steed. They spoke endlessly with Sarah's occasional comment or question.

Haben and I caught up on lost time. Haben and my late husband had been best friends. They served together in the King's guard. Haben wanted to know about my time in the East. It was lovely to remember those years. Garth and I had been so happy. We were seeing new places, meeting exciting, intelligent people and having our eye and minds opened to all sorts of new ideas.

James was so happy to be free that he refused to walk with us, instead he made lazy circles in the sky overhead.

"Theresa?" King William called from the other side of Haben. "Would you consider a royal appointment? Farloft and I have been talking and we think you would make an excellent adviser to the crown."

"That is a weighty appointment, Your Majesty," I answered. I think I may have blushed, even at my age.

"Your healing powers are a great gift and one that I would like to have in my castle," William continued. "You were the most assistance to my father in his last days. You could have Laval's quarters and access to any of his notes and journals."

"Perhaps you could learn to be a wizard," Farloft said with a wink at me.

"I could only consent if I was allowed to continue to practice healing for the villagers and the forest folk," I said.

"And the animals," Farloft added. He was really getting a kick out of this. No doubt he was behind it all.

"Done!" King William announced. "And of course Sarah will be welcome at all times. We have plenty of room in the castle."

Sarah smiled. Farloft winked again at me. Haben chuckled. I just rolled my eyes. Where would this all lead?

- THE END -

ABOUT THE AUTHOR

Theresa Snyder is a member in good standing of The Society of Enlightened Dragonologist. She and fellow founder Cheri Matthynssens, created the Society to assist their respective dragons, Keensight and Farloft, in their desire to have humans relate to dragons as intelligent beings rather than the killers they are often portrayed as in book and films.

Theresa loves to travel, but makes her home in Oregon where her elder father and she share a home and the maintenance of the resident cat, wild birds, squirrels, garden and occasional dragon houseguest.

Cover by Sarah Hyndshaw

AUTHOR'S NOTE

Thank you for reading.
I hope you enjoyed James and Farloft's adventure.
Please consider leaving a review on Amazon, Smashwords, Goodreads, or any other social media to help other readers find the story.

Made in the USA
Charleston, SC
07 July 2014